BY **EVE BUNTING**

MY BACKPACK

ILLUSTRATED BY **MARYANN COCCA-LEFFLER**

BOYDS MILLS PRESS

Y-
Picture
BUN

To our backpack girls -
Anna, Dana, Tony
and Erin.
Love Grandma.

To
Nicholas
Thinking of
you!!
Love,
Auntie
Maryann

Text copyright © 1997 by Eve Bunting
Illustrations copyright © 1997 by Maryann Cocca-Leffler
All rights reserved

Published by Caroline House
Boyds Mills Press, Inc.
A Highlights Company
815 Church Street
Honesdale, Pennsylvania 18431
Printed in Mexico

Publisher Cataloging-in-Publication Data
Bunting, Eve.
    My backpack / by Eve Bunting ; illustrated by Maryann Cocca-Leffler.
—1st ed.
[32]p. : col.ill. ; cm.
Summary :A boy discovers how many wonderful things he can fit in his backpack.
ISBN 1-56397-433-9
1. Children—Juvenile literature—Fiction. [1. Children—Fiction.] I. Cocca-Leffler, Maryann, ill. II. Title.
        [E]—dc20   1997   AC   CIP
Library of Congress Catalog Card Number 96-83934

First edition, 1997
Book designed by Tim Gillner and Maryann Cocca-Leffler
The text of this book is set in 24-point Gill Sans Bold.
The illustrations are done in gouache, colored pencils, and collage.

10 9 8 7 6 5 4 3 2 1

My backpack's big,
my backpack's blue,
my backpack's very nearly new.
Grandma sent it in the mail.
She bought it at a garage sale.
She says by now I'm big enough
to fill it with important stuff.

I'll put my teddy bear inside.
He'll like a little backpack ride.

Here's my train.
I'll take my blocks.
I'll take my brother's baseball socks.
I think I'll take his catcher's mitt—
he keeps it soft with lots of spit.

My mother hangs her
keys up high,
but I can reach them if I try.
I'll take a cookie and a spare—
one for me and one for bear.
There's lots of room,
I could take more.
OK! I guess I could take four.

Dad leaves his glasses everywhere.
I see them sitting on his chair.
I'll put them carefully away.
His glasses won't get lost today!

I like this television thing.
You push it and it makes a ping.
Cartoons come on and
   sometimes news.
I think I'll take my mother's shoes.

PING

I'll take my kitty and his dish.
It smells a bit of last
    night's fish.
I'll take the dustpan and
    the broom—
No, not the broom,
    there isn't room.
My backpack weighs
    an awful lot.
All these important
    things I've got!

MEOW

I'll push the screen door,
    hold it wide.
"See, kitty, see?
    It's nice outside."

When Mom and Dad see
    what I've done,
they'll *know* they have a
    clever son!
"He learned so quickly!"
    Mom will say.
"He only got it yesterday!"

"**M**om, I've lost my catcher's mitt.
Of course I've really looked for it.
My socks have gone,
    that's what I said.
Of course I've looked beneath
    the bed."

"I left my glasses on my chair.
Now I can't find them anywhere."

" **M**y shoes have vanished, they were here.
How could they simply disappear?
What else is missing?
Look around!"

"Don't bother, Mom.
The burglar's found!"

"He took my keys!"

"He took my socks!"

"He took the television box."

"I've got my glasses."

"Here's my mitt—
     Oh, gross! He's added extra spit!"

"Here's one shoe and here's the other. Say you're sorry to your mother!"

"I *know* you didn't understand.
OK, OK, I'll hold your hand.
OK, OK, I'll carry you.
I'll carry you and kitty, too."

Grandma would be pleased to see
my backpack all filled
up with ME!